Ben Balloon and Friends

Mary Bowyer

Ben Balloon and Friends

iUniverse books may be ordered through booksellers or by contacting:

iUniverse
1663 Liberty Drive
Bloomington, IN 47403
www.iuniverse.com
1-800-Authors (1-800-288-4677)

ISBN: 978-1-5320-9841-3 (sc)
ISBN: 978-1-5320-9842-0 (e)

Library of Congress Control Number: 2020905804

Print information available on the last page.

iUniverse rev. date: 08/06/2020

Ben Balloon and Friends

Ben Balloon

Ben Balloon was very sad, for he was flat as could be.
Not nice and round and full of air like proper balloons should be.
Every day he glanced in the mirror to see if he'd got fat
And every day he sadly saw that he was still as flat.

Then one bright day Anne Airful came and blew him up so round,
That now he floats ten thousand million feet above the ground.
He hobnobs with the clouds and stars, they tell him lovely tales,
And if you look 'way, 'way up high, you'll see him as he sails.

Jennifer Soames

Jennifer Soames
Loved to write poems.
She wrote in the trees,
And she wrote on the breeze.
She wrote at the dawn
And wrote on the lawn.
In a bed of bright flowers,
For hours and hours.
Jennifer Soames
Loved to write poems.

The Talking Towel

I rubbed my hands on the Talking Towel,
Was I surprised when he let out a howl,
And told me that he had something to say
And could I kindly dry my hands another day.

He talked on and on about his life
About his kids and about his wife
To tell the truth he's talking yet
And my poor hands, they're still all wet.

Cuddly Bear

Cuddly Bear went to the store
To buy herself a bow
To place atop her cuddly fur
So she would look just so.

But on arriving at the store
There were no bows in sight,
Just one small pair of roller skates
Which filled her with delight.

So 'stead of being Cuddly Bear
Whose looks compared to none,
She was Cuddly Bear on roller skates
(Which was a lot more fun!)

Daisy Duck

Daisy duck said "quack,quack, quack,
I'll swim around the pond and back,
I'll swim real slow come back and then
I'll swim around the pond again."

Shoop, Shoop, Noodle Soup

Shoop, shoop
Noodle soup,
Drink it when you start to droop.
Scoop the noodles with a scoop,
Shoop, shoop,
Noodle soup.

It's good for slurping right out loud
To quite impress a great big crowd.
It's good for sprinkling at your dad
(Although he might get slightly mad.)
Shoop, shoop
Noodle soup.
Drink it when you start to droop.

Chatter-to-Ya

Chatter-to-ya, scatter-to-ya,
Tell me, what's it matter to ya?
That I caught the biggest bear,
That ever lumbered anywhere?
That I caught the biggest fish
To ever sit on any dish?
That I eat my meals on wheels
And never walk but on my heels?
Chatter-to-ya, scatter-to-ya,
Tell me, what's it matter to ya?

Toodle

Toodle-o Poodle-o
Looked like a noodle-o
Even though she was a doggy,
She ran and she danced
She galloped and pranced
With her best friend,
Frederico the froggy.

She climbed up tall trees,
And she swayed in the breeze
And she filled herself with doggy candy
And after a day
Of jumping and play
She found herself feeling quite dandy.

Toodle-O Poodle-o
Looked like a noodle-o
Even though she was a doggy.
She ran and she danced
She galloped and pranced
With her best friend,
Frederico the froggy.

Sammy Seal

Sammy Seal lay basking in the sun
His day of chasing fish and such was done.
He heard a gentle splash of water
Spied a fish and nearly caught her.
When she spoke up (from safely on the run).

"Oh, Sammy Seal, why do you chase me?
To eat me up is just to waste me.
Let's bring this killing to an end
And let me be your little friend."

Sammy pondered the small fish's wish
(He'd never before been friends with a fish).
But she was so sweet, with a big smile so grand
He put out his fin to shake her sweet hand.

Now they swim fin in hand over Life's lovely seas
And Sam and the fish are both very pleased.
For they've learned that the problems of fishship and menship
Can be solved by one thing and one thing only: Friendship.

The Little Pig

The little pig
Did dance a jig
Quite upside down
In his pigsty.
He danced with Mortimer, the cat
With Dick, the horse
And Bert, the fly.
He danced till he could dance no more
Then said, "Oh, what a pig am I."

Superman Stan

Superman Stan
Was a great big strong man.
His red cape he wore with a grin.
He wore it outside
And he wore it to play
And he wore it when mom tucked him in.

I Met Mr. Bear

I met Mr. Bear,
He was hungry and mean.
He said, "I would eat you.
But you're really too lean.
Here's a chocolate éclair,
Make you fit for a bear."
But I said, "N–N–No, I really must go.
I really would try it
But I'm on a strict diet,
I get th–thinner each day."
And I scooted away.

Timoctopus Octopus

Timoctopus Octopus
Had eight long arms,
He sang to the fishes
With all of his charms.
The fish loved his song
And they shouted—More! More!
So he bowed quite politely
And did an encore.

Bobby Blanket

Bobby Blanket keeps me warm
He's my best friend in a thunderstorm.
I tell him all my joys and fears
He's always there to lend an ear.
And when I wiggle or I wuggle
He's always very glad to snuggle.

The Sheep

Once there was a sheep
Who mumbled, "Bleep, bleep, bleep
I'm stuck here in this pen
And must get out again.

I need so to be free
(And drink a cup of tea.)
So happy I would be,
The whole world I could see."

Then Dino Dog walked by
And said, "I'm going to try
To let you out, sweet sheep
But first you get some sleep."

Next morn the sheep awoke
And found his bars all broke
The two began to dance
Forever did they prance.

Little House

Little House sat on the hill
Feeling very sad and lonesome
For his owners had just moved away
And the weeds outside, they sure had grown some.

"Oh, woe is me," cried Little House,
"What is to become of me?
My stairs are creaking,
No one loves me
And the ants have eaten some of me.

My plaster's falling from the ceiling
My gates are getting worn and rusty.
It sure gives me an awful feeling
To say nothing of my smell, so musty."

HEY, try a bite of this house!

His chimney shook with unshed tears
Then he just broke right down and cried,
When suddenly a Lovely Lady
Singing softly stepped inside.

"I'll fix you up, you precious house,"
She very sweetly, softly said.
Oh! Little House was so excited
That night he couldn't stay in bed

She cleaned and mopped
And fixed and pruned
And swept the floors with sweeps so sweeply.
Now Little House is very gay
For Lovely Lady loves him deeply.

What's a Moekling?

"What's a moekling?" asked the king.
"A moekling's part "moek" and part "ling."
A moekling's small and loves to sing.
Or a moekling's big with golden wings.

A moekling has a ruddy snout,
And loves to laugh and roam about.
Among the trees, so you can see,
He's quite a lot like you and me."

"I think I see now," said the king.
"I'd love to have my own moekling."
"They're not for having, no siree,
For moeklings must always be free.

But if at night you close your eyes
And point your finger to the skies,
Your own moekling with furry head
Will cuddle with you in your bed."

Iguana

I spy a little shy iguana
To see and pet him,
Yes, I wanna.

He follows me where-e'r I go,
In hottest sun
And coldest snow.

I spy a little shy iguana
To see and pet him,
Yes, I wanna.

Tony Turtle

Tony Turtle was strolling through the garden
When he 'spied
A great big rock that had a hole
That he could hide inside.

Mom Turtle will never find me here, he thought.
I'll have my wishes
Of never having to eat my broccoli
Or help with dinner dishes.

So Tony Turtle crawled inside
But soon afterward he thought
Of how Mom Turtle stroked his shell
(He sure liked that a lot).

And how she patted his head
Before he went to bed, and kissed it,
He used to think it kind of dumb
But now he sort of missed it.

He thought of Daddy Turtle
And the stories he would tell
Of brave, strong turtles long ago.
Those stories sure were swell.

So Tony Turtle ran on home
To the sweet home that was his,
Fast as a lightning thunderbolt
(For a small turtle, that is).

Squink-ily Pink-ily

Squink-ily Pink-ily
So loved to wink-ily.
She winked at giraffes
At sweet, newborn calves
She winked at big noodles
She winked at small poodles
At rambunctious froggies
Hilarious hoggies
And winked the night away.
Squink-ily Pink-ily
So loved to wink-ily.

Silly Willy

Silly Willy went to Philly.
Maybe he is still-y there.
For Philly has the neatest music
And the greatest county fair.

Silly Willy rode a red horse
There at Philly's county fair,
And Silly Willy won't step down
From Philly's filly, will he?

Little Piggy

Little Piggy ran and jumped,
Into the furniture he bumped.
He did a headstand on his snout,
He smiled and laughed and twirled about.

Little Tommy was delighted,
But Mommy was a little frighted.
"I don't know," she said to Dad,
"To clean up, what a time I've had."

But Little Tommy begged and pleaded,
So to his wishes Mom acceded.
The Piggy lived there ever after,
And the house was always filled with laughter.

MOMMY, DADDY, CAN WE KEEP HIM?

Tic-y, Tac-y, Toe-y

Tic-y, tac-y, toe-y,
I have a friend named Joey,
And everywhere we go-y,
Through wind or rain or snow-y,
If it's sunny or it's blow-y,
Together's how we go-y,
Just me and my friend, Joey,
Tic-y, tac-y, toe-y.

Marsulio Minnipus

Marsulio Minnipus
Rode on a city bus,
Gazed out the window
As the sunlight did glint-o.
Rode past the lake,
Munching on cake.
Marsulio Minnipus
Rode on a city bus.

Nelson Noodle

Nelson Noodle was so flat
As flat as he could be,
Upon a sea of soup he sat
And muttered gloomily.

"I'd love to run and jump and step
Instead of lying here,
If I could have a little pep
How full I'd be of cheer.

To jump and run and dance and sing
That is my fondest wish,
To roller skate, all full of zing
Not lie here in this dish.

Then Granny Noodle did appear
From noodleland on high,
She said, "You're perfect as you are
So, Nelson, don't ask why

You cannot run and skip and roll
Just like an ol' French poodle,
Just swim around in this fine bowl
And be proud to be a noodle."

Time Was

Time was when alligators flew
And ponies said "Cockadoodle-doo"
And dogs could sing
And mice had wings
There was a time when pigs went "mew."

But nowadays the cats "meow"
A mooing sound comes from a cow
The young birds sing
The geese have wings
I think the world is mixed up now.

Sing, Sing, Little Bird

Sing, sing, little bird.
Sing, sing little bird.
Your song is so special,
It needs to be heard.
Your song is so lovely,
A song without words.
Sing, sing, little bird.
Sing, sing, little bird.

Stumble-bee Bumblebee

Stumble-bee Bumblebee
Couldn't walk straight.
Walked thru the flowers
With an unwieldy gait.
He felt, oh so different
From most other bees,
He said to the queen bee
"Please help me, queen, please."

The queen bee made up
A bumblebee potion,
Out of seaweed and shells
That she found at the ocean.
She gave it to Stumble
And to his great surprise
He not only walks straight,
He flies to the skies.

The Sweet Little Rowboat

The sweet little rowboat
Was lost at sea.
"Oh, my," she cried
"What will happen to me?"
She got ate by a whale
And got stuck in his tale,
But got blown out his mouth
By the next gusty gale.
She rowed and she rowed,
She at last reached the shore.
"It's lagoons from now on,"
She said—forevermore.

AH - CHOO!

Terrific

I feel terrific
Quite splentific
Almost feel that I could fly.
I feel so yummy
Filled my tummy
With a cherry pie on rye.

I feel so, so good
Nothing's no good
Feel like diving in a pool.
My teacher told us,
Smiled and told us,
That tomorrow there's no school.

Clickety-Plickety Rickety-Rum

Clickety-plickety rickety-rum
Bang on the cymbals, beat on the drum,
A dancing elf will surely come
Clickety-plickety rickety-rum.

Ode to Mostachioli

Mostachoodle, mostachoodle,
What a funny kind of noodle.
Looks a little like a poodle,
Looks a little like a flute-al.
You can draw or you can doodle
A terrific mostachoodle,
But the best thing you can do-dle
With your special mostachoodle
Is to eat it,
You can't beat it,
It's a most delicious foodle.

Johnny Jello

Johnny Jello couldn't jiggle
Not even the slightest wiggle
He sat in his bowl, quite an unhappy fellow
For if Jell-O can't jiggle, it hardly is Jell-O.

Then one day, the Jiggling Godmother walked past
Saw Johnny and set him to jiggling real fast
Now Johnny not only wiggles and jiggles
He's so very happy, that he even giggles.

Minula Mousie

Minula Mousie sat and wondered,
Why it rained and poured and thundered.
She sat for hours pondering
The flash and noise that rainstorms bring.
"It must be giant mice above
A 'fighting with their boxing gloves
That makes the thunder groan and growl
And clap and shriek and shout and howl.
And when one giant mousie wins,
Exactly then—the rain begins.
The losing mousie sits and cries
And pours down teardrops from the skies,
Till once again Dame Sun does rise
To dry his red and swollen eyes.

Pimila Stimila

Pimila Stimila
So loved to Swim-ila.
She swam in the ocean
So full of emotion.
She swam at the beach
The shoreline to reach.
She kicked up her feet
Where the waves and sand meet.
Pimila Stimila
So loved to swim-ila.

Twinky T'wosy

Twinky T'wosy
Has a nosey
Longer than a row of darts.
And when she runs around the block
Her nose gets home before *she* starts.

Pistachio Pillow

Pistachio Pillow sat on the bed
Patiently waiting for little Tim's head.
He let out a sigh
When he heard Timmy cry
"One more story, Mom, please!"
"That's the tenth one she read!"
An impatient and lonesome Pistachio said.

Harry Horsie

Harry Horsie
Said "Of cours-ie
I will take a little trot
With my shadow
Cross the meadow,
A sedentary horse I'm not.

Said Henry Horsie
Wait a bit
I'll join you and
We'll play a game
We'll gallop and we'll canter,
And "hip hip hooray," exclaim.

The two had such fun playing there
They danced and pranced the day away
"Oh what great fun," the horsies said,
"It's been a splendid, magic day."

There Was a Little Butterfly

There was a little butterfly
Who wanted so to reach the sky.
All day she'd flap her wings and try,
But only climbed a few feet high.
Then suddenly there came a word
Of wisdom from a little bird.
He said, "My friend, don't just aspire
To fly higher and yet higher,
But make the most of each inch flown.
Your flight is not only your own,
But visit with each tree and flower
And bring each one a happy hour.
Then the butterfly flew here and there
Spreading kind words everywhere,
Leaving seeds of caring deeds
With trees, with flowers, even weeds.
She cared no more to reach the skies
The butterfly had grown so wise.
She'd gained real joy, she'd gained real bliss
By sharing love and happiness.

Pauletta Anne Lin

Pauletta Anne Lin
Was ever so thin
She fit through the slot
That the mail would go in.
She fit through the rails
On the banister, too
And before she ate breakfast
She vanished from view.

Mommy Mousie

Mommy Mousie had a tail,
Longer than a city mile.
All her little mousie babes,
Jumped rope with it, it made her smile.

Timothy Tree

Timothy Tree
Wanted to see
Far as could be.
Timothy Tree.
He stretched his long neck
But he felt like a speck
Wedged between the tall trees,
A boring small tree.
He so felt like crying
but he never stopped trying.
He reached to the sky
And then – my oh my -
His leaves were unfurled
He could see the whole world.

China Cup and Chandelier

China Cup and Chandelier
Engaged in conversation.
Said Chandelier to China Cup,
"I need a sweet libation."

Said China Cup to Chandelier
"Come hither, drink my brew.
And if you do not mind too much
I'll ask a favor of you.

I'm sitting in the kitchen, dark
Without a bit of light.
Please shine on me, a tiny spark
To brighten up my night."

"Most certainly," said Chandelier,
"You are my friend and so,
I'll shine for you the brightest light
To set your heart aglow."

He shone his light, and sipped his brew
(Which filled him with delight)
And watched as China fell asleep
Then, soft, turned out the light.

Little Gnat

There was a very little gnat
Who ate a cake and grew quite fat,
He ate three pies and grew immense,
He couldn't fit beneath the fence.
To get on home to his gnat nest
(and his sweet Mom, the very best).
He wanted very bad to see her
So he came up with an ideer.

He threw away his cakes and pies,
He threw them high, they touched the skies.
For three days he ate beans and rice
Till he shrunk to his former size.

Then underneath the fence he went
His taste for pies completely spent,
He was, as you are surely guessin'
A little gnat who'd learned his lesson.

Wimsy Won-sy

Wimsy Won-sy
Had such fun-sy
Reading fairy tales
'Bout snakes and dogs and
elephants
'Bout pirate ships and whales.

'Bout kitty-cats
And great, big hats
And dragons breathing fire,
'Bout flowers and 'bout honeybees
Of birds upon the wire.

Wimsy Won-sy
Had such fun-sy
Reading fairy tales
'Bout snakes and dogs and elephants
'Bout pirate ships and whales.

Plink, Plink, Pitter, Patter

Plink, plink,
Pitter, Patter
Raindrops kiss my window sill.
Outside the world is washed all clean,
Inside it's peaceful and it's still.

Plink, plink,
Pitter, patter.
Raindrops, nighttime company
To green the grass
And red the rose
And play a lovely song for me.

Plink, plink,
Pitter, Patter
Raindrops kiss my window sill.
Outside the world is washed all clean,
Inside it's peaceful and it's still.

Printed in the USA
CPSIA information can be obtained
at www.ICGtesting.com
JSHW071250290224
58157JS00020B/247